D1305717

For George, love Aunty Lu —L.R.

For Cohen and Dexter —K.H.

Lucy Rowland  Katy Halford

There's No Such Thing As...
ELVES

CHRISTMAS
DECORATIONS

Scholastic Press · New York

"There's **no such thing** as **elves**, you know,"

my best friend said last night.

Today I'll go **exploring**

just to see if she is right.

I've got my list –

I've checked it twice.

There's **such** a lot to do!

And so much **searching** to be done, so

could YOU help me, too?

"There's **no such thing** as elves," Mom said.

But Santa **needs** his elves!

I looked through all our cupboards,

then I searched on all our shelves.

"There's **no such thing** as elves," they said.

A workshop's where they'd hide.

I checked in ours quite carefully
but there were **none** inside.

There's **no such thing** as **elves,** you see.

But maybe in the **shed?**

I couldn't find an elf there . . .

just my little trike instead.

"There's **no such thing** as elves," I hear.

But **ponds** make lovely homes.

No elves as far as I could see . . .

just Mommy's garden gnomes.

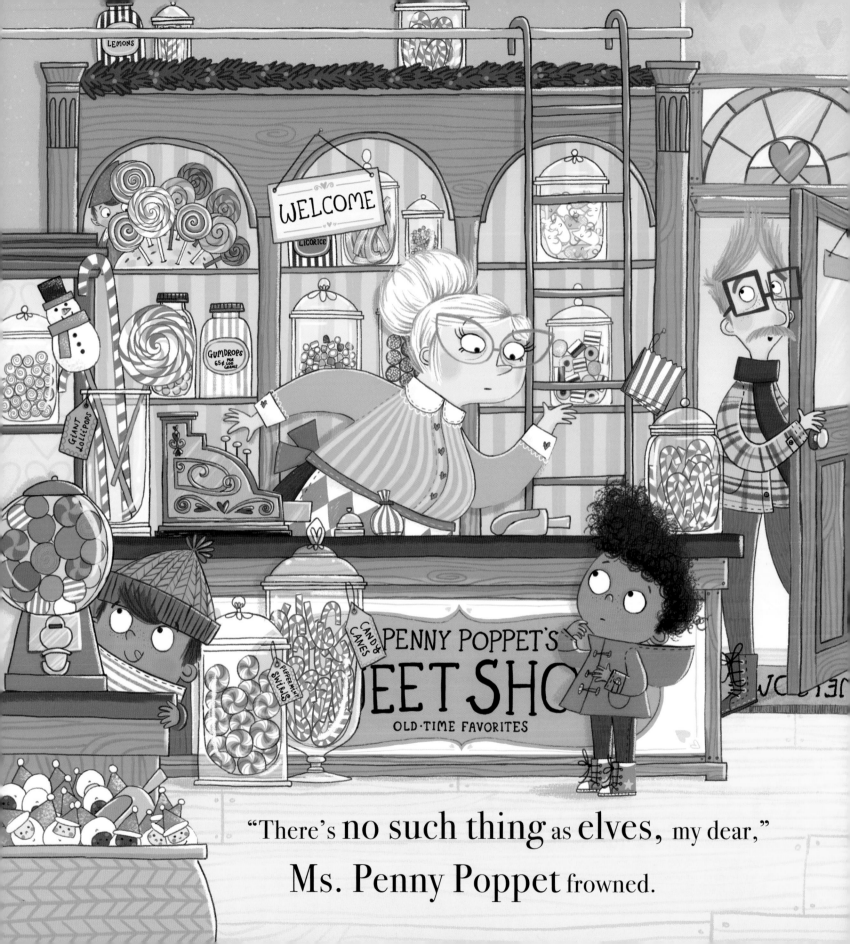

"There's **no such thing** as elves, my dear,"
Ms. Penny Poppet frowned.

But I know elves **love** candy canes.

I had a look around.

"There's **no such thing** as **elves**, my boy,"

the smiling shop man sighed.

I thought I saw one in the back.

I had a peep inside.

"Oh, we believe in elves,"
whispered the reindeer at the fence.

"We saw one just this morning,

but we haven't seen him since."

There's **no such thing** as elves, I guess.

But . . . maybe when it **snows**?

I even spoke to Santa but . . .

he said his elves weren't there.

"Oh, **there** you are!" my best friend calls.

"I've looked all around for you."

"There's **no such thing** as elves," I sob.

"You're right.

It must be TRUE."

She puts her arm around me, and before we turn to go,

we see a shiny **Christmas star**

and then it starts to snow.

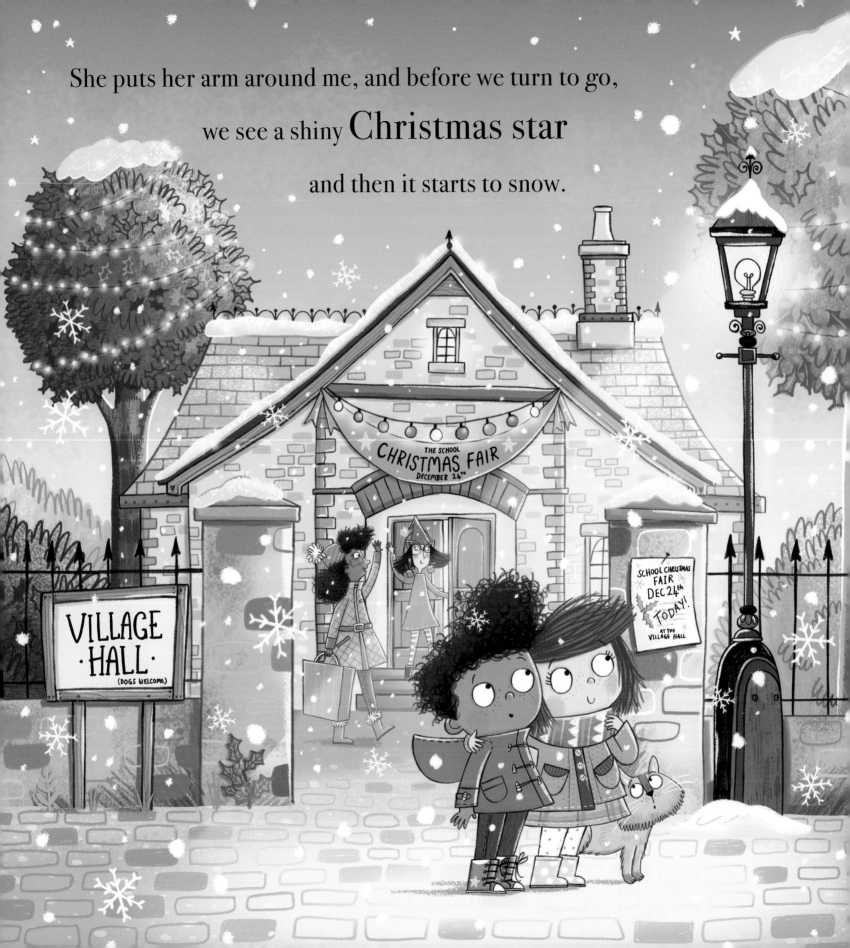

But, on our way back home again . . .

a frost is in the air . . .

the snowflakes start to sparkle and . . .

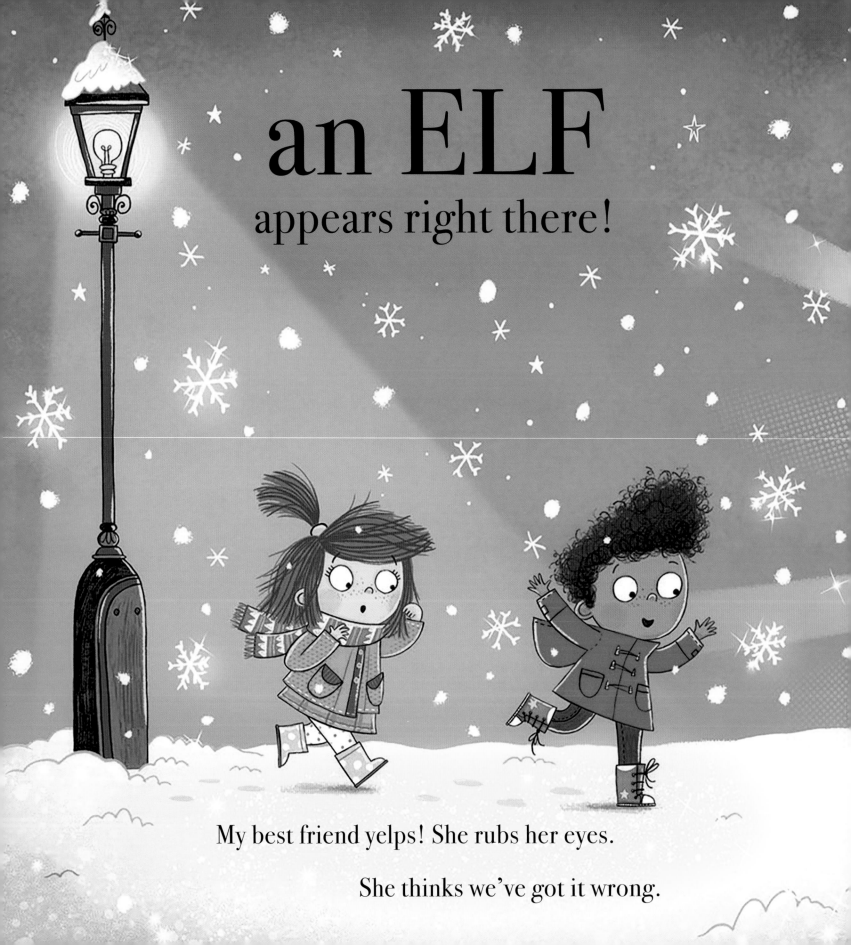

an ELF
appears right there!

My best friend yelps! She rubs her eyes.

She thinks we've got it wrong.

But . . . there ARE such things as elves, you see!

I knew it all along!